# Young Kangaroo

# Young Kangaroo

## Margaret Wise Brown

*Illustrated by* Jennifer Dewey

Hyperion Books for Children
New York

To the wildlife of Australia
—J. D.

Printed in Hong Kong.
For information address Hyperion Books for Children,
114 Fifth Avenue, New York, New York 10011.

First Edition
1 3 5 7 9 10 8 6 4 2

Library of Congress Cataloging-in-Publication Data
Brown, Margaret Wise
Young kangaroo / Margaret Wise Brown;
illustrated by Jennifer Dewey—1st ed.
p.   cm.
Summary: A tiny kangaroo is born and moves
into his mother's pouch, where he grows big enough
to be interested in the world around him long before he
actually leaves her pouch to investigate further.
ISBN 1-56282-409-0 (trade)
—ISBN 1-56282-410-4 (library)
1. Kangaroos—Juvenile fiction.   [1. Kangaroos—Fiction.
2. Animals—Infancy—Fiction.]
I. Dewey, Jennifer, ill.   II. Title.
PZ10.3.B7656Yo   1993   [E]—dc20   92-54866   CIP   AC

The artwork for each picture is prepared using colored pencil on vellum.
This book is set in 16-point Horley Old Style.

# Young Kangaroo

It was a little kangaroo—how little you would never believe. It was about one inch long when it was born—the size of a baby mouse, the size of a child's toe, the size of a joey, a baby kangaroo.

Then, blind and naked and helpless as it was, it began climbing arm over arm through the fur on its mother's stomach, up toward the pouch that was to be its own dark nursery for about the first seven months of its life.

It took three minutes to make that first journey, arm over arm, from hair to hair, through a soft woolly forest of fur. At one point the baby kangaroo got caught in the fur. His feet were all tangled in hairs and he could not go on. The mother kangaroo leaned slowly down and nudged him on his way. Then he started crawling again, and in time he got there, safe in the mother kangaroo's pouch.

Deep in the pocket of the pouch, the baby kangaroo found his mother's breast, and he hung on for dear life. For the next few months, that was all he had to do. Later on he would grow a little fur coat of his own, he would have a little kangaroo shape of his own, and when the time came he would come peeking out at the world about him.

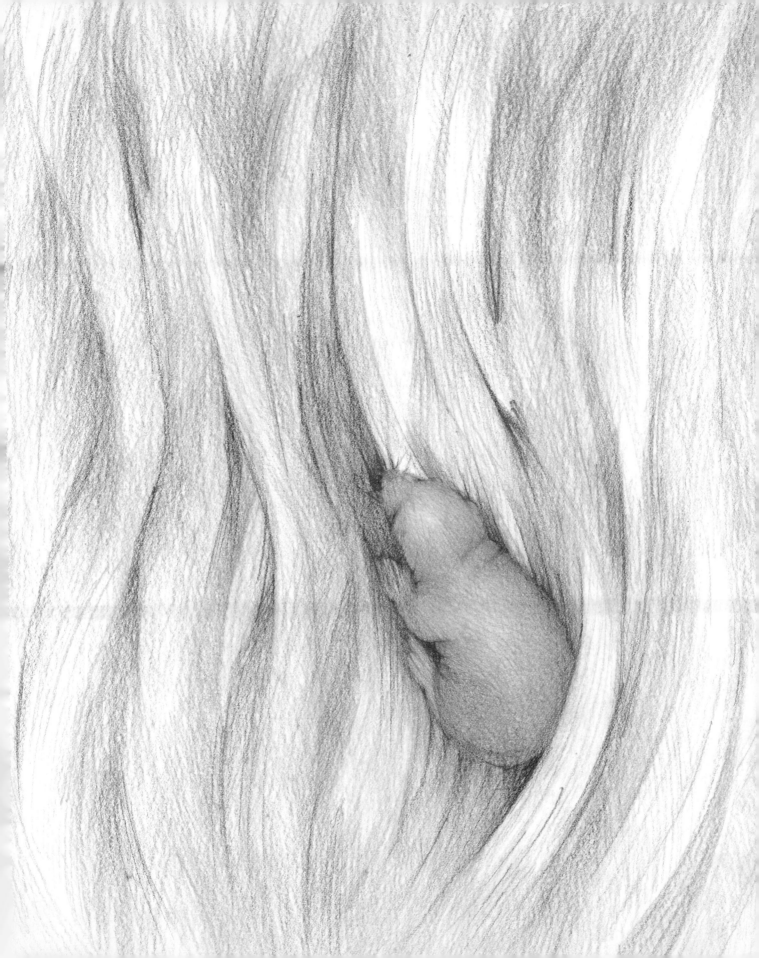

But that time was still to come, and
in the meantime his mother went hopping
about over the grassy plains of Australia.
And to see her bounding along, clearing
high bushes and fences with her long
kangaroo tail streaming out behind her,
no one would ever have suspected that
in her pouch she harbored a little
growing kangaroo.

But the little fellow in her pouch knew that he was there. And all this time he was growing and growing, bigger and bigger. The first month he grew as big as a baby squirrel; the next month he was the size of a puppy dog. And when he was about as big as a small monkey, in the fourth month, he came peeking out.

He got tired of riding around in the dark. Where was he going? Why was everything still and quiet some of the time, while at other times everything was moving?

He couldn't see yet, but slowly and cautiously he stuck his little nose out and sniffed the air. And as he sniffed he found that the air changed. The more he sniffed, the more it changed. Sometimes it was cold and damp, sometimes it was sweet and dry, sometimes it was just empty of smell. Sometimes he smelled other kangaroos. They smelled big and warm. Sometimes he smelled sweet acacia and spicy eucalyptus trees, sometimes the prickly dry smell after rain.

It was all very curious—because it was always changing. The little kangaroo began to suspect that there was something in the world beyond his own nose that he ought to find out about.

And so one day he followed his nose, and his eyes peeked out. His newly opened eyes were blinded by a blaze of light. He pulled his head back into the pouch, back into the familiar darkness that didn't hurt his eyes. But that first blaze of light had been exciting to him, as it is to all young animals when they first open their eyes. And the little joey popped his head out again and again.

Once when he popped his head out, it was dark—not as dark as his mother's pouch, but there was no white blaze of light to blind his eyes. He looked up and saw little far-off pricks of light above him. The stars were far away, and they didn't blind his eyes like the blaze of daylight. They were little lights that he could look at.

The little joey knew through his eyes what his nose had first told him. The world was full of changes—changing smells and changing lights. What was behind the changes he would some day find out.

Fast as his hair and teeth and bones grew, his curiosity grew faster. Soon his eyes began to focus.

Tall blurs went by him as his mother leaped along, little blurs went by him, and blurs that smelled like other kangaroos leaped about him. And gradually in all this blur he saw trees and bushes and the other kangaroos, and the blurs became living and growing things. The baby kangaroo could see.

From the time the little kangaroo could see all the trees, bushes, far horizons, and other kangaroos—from the time he could begin to see what it was that he smelled—the little kangaroo was busy every seeing minute of the day. But most of the time he was very busy sleeping and eating and just growing, for it takes a lot of sleeping and eating and peering about and wondering to make any little animal grow—a child, a kitten, or a kangaroo.

And then one day when his mother took flying leaps over green bushes that brushed past the baby joey's face, he reached out his little paw and grabbed a green leaf. He put it in his mouth and left it there and played with it. He liked it so much he swallowed it. From then on the little joey was nibbling at everything his quick little paws could grab.

There were five ways of finding out what something was, the little joey learned. You could smell what it smelled like. You could see what it looked like. You could feel what it felt like. You could hear what it sounded like. Most things, the little joey discovered, were quiet, and, anyway, he was more interested in putting things in his mouth and tasting what they tasted like.

If he liked what something tasted like and it was good for him, he felt good. If it wasn't good for him, he felt bad—he felt bad in his stomach. The things that made him feel good he grew to know by their smell and by the look of them, and he grabbed them as often as he could see them and reach out for them—green buds and tender little leaves and soft thorns.

And then one day he reached out so far to grab at some bright green grass blades that he pulled himself right out of the pouch. And there he was, tumbling on the ground, apart from his mother. He didn't stay that way long! He was frightened to death. And, quick as the flight of an Australian bird, certain as a streak of lightning, he scrambled back and dived headfirst into his mother's pouch, and he didn't come peeking out of it again until the next day.

But the next day, much to his surprise, the first thing he did was to grab at a tuft of green, and out he came again on the ground, and back he dived into the pouch.

Before long he had pulled himself out again, and this time he stayed a little longer and looked about him. He was standing in the grass on the world. He was standing on his own two feet. He nibbled at the grass and it tasted good. He listened carefully and he heard the wind in the grass. He could hear the wind, but he couldn't taste it or see it. He saw a black bug with shiny wings.

This was the world of Australia. Great plains of waving green grass grew all about him. As far as you could look there was distance, and about him, where the little joey could see them, were other kangaroos—great, warm, woolly animals, propped against their tails and twitching their noses.

When the little joey had been on the
ground often enough to feel at home there,
he sat up and leaned back against his tail
and twitched his nose just like any other
kangaroo, and his loose gentle paws hung
down like the idle paws of a bunny.

At this age the little joey was not any
bigger than a beaver. He was smaller than
the bushes. He had to stretch his baby neck
way up to get at the tender top leaves of
the bushes. His mother never helped him.
She knew that the longer he stretched, the
stronger he would grow.

Traveling around with his mother was like flying. She took great bounds that cleared the earth and sent her through the air, high above fences and bushes. She could easily have jumped right over a horse or a man if she had met one.

One day she did meet a man—a man with a gun. She got so excited she ran toward him, instead of away from him, and jumped right over him. He was so surprised he fell flat on his face, and his gun went off, low along the ground.

But out on the plains the kangaroos seldom meet other animals. There are no meat-eating animals native to the continent of Australia except wild dogs called dingoes. Most of the other animals eat grass, so dingoes and men are the only enemies of the bounding kangaroo.

The young kangaroo, though he could not bite, could kick the daylights out of his enemies with his powerful hind foot or rip them open with the long razorlike claw of his third hind toe. He seldom used his little limp forepaws, but he could use them also, if he wanted to.

One day he was bounding along inside his mother's pouch when he heard her heart begin to beat faster. His own little heart began to beat faster. He peeked out of the pouch, and then he heard barking and baying. The grasses and the bushes and the trees were all rushing by beneath him as his mother leaped along. She seemed to be flying over everything as she went tearing along. And the sound of the dingoes grew louder and nearer in his ears.

His mother's heart began to thump wildly and then to thud. Suddenly, as they sailed over a clump of bushes, she reached down with her front paws and threw him into a bush. Before he could prop himself up and look around, she had gone and he was alone—alone in the middle of a bush.

A great snuffing and padding of paws went past him. It was the dingoes that were chasing his mother, but he didn't know that. He didn't know that his weight in his mother's pouch had slowed her down so much that, if she had not thrown him into a bush, she would have been caught by the dingoes and they both would have been killed. But, by throwing him into a bush, she had saved him and she had saved herself.

Only how could a little kangaroo know that? All he knew was that his mother wasn't there. For the first time in his life he was alone. Alone in a bush. Silence fell about him after the dingoes had passed, and he was alone in the world.

Alone. It was awful, as he had never been alone before. It was like the sound behind the wind. At first the little kangaroo couldn't stand it, and he fought to get out of the bush. He whimpered and he wailed. But then he got more used to it and grew tired in his grief. After a while he whimpered himself into a cold little sleep.

His mother, with no little kangaroo in her pouch to weigh her down, easily got away from the dingoes. Then she returned to the brush to look for her tossed-out baby. But when she got there, it was dark, and she could not see him. There were so many bushes. The air was cold and dry, and, sniff as she may, she couldn't smell him. By that time he had cried himself to sleep, so she couldn't hear him. But she knew he was somewhere nearby, so she waited there all night for some sign from him.

Late that night the little kangaroo woke up. Stars were cold above him. The wind was cold, and the branches of the bush were cold. He remembered—he was all alone. He whimpered a thin little whimper.

And then, not far off, he heard a familiar snuffle, and his mother came leaping up to him. She lifted him up in her forepaws and put him back headfirst into her pouch, where he was dark and safe and warm.

Back in the pouch the little kangaroo closed his eyes. Near him his mother's heart was beating slowly—thump, thump, thump. He was home. He was with his mother, and his little wild heartbeats came more slowly. Behind closed eyes, sleep came to him again—only this time a long, warm sleep, full of tender grasses and little kangaroo dreams.